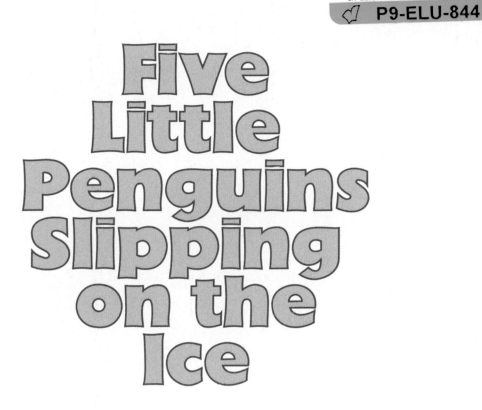

Five Little Penguins Slipping on the Ice

To Mutti, Lopey, Nancy, and Julia

— S.M.

To Andy and Andrea

— L.B.

ISBN 0-439-46577-X

Text copyright © 2002 by Steve Metzger.
Illustrations copyright © 2002 by Laura Bryant.
All rights reserved.   Published by Scholastic Inc.
SCHOLASTIC and associated logos are trademarks and/or registered trademarks of Scholastic Inc.

28 27 26 25 24   19 20 21 22/0

Printed in the U.S.A.
First printing, December 2002

Five Little Penguins Slipping on the Ice

by Steve Metzger
Illustrated by Laura Bryant

SCHOLASTIC INC.
New York   Toronto   London   Auckland   Sydney
Mexico City   New Delhi   Hong Kong   Buenos Aires

Five little penguins slipping on the ice.

One fell down. "Ouch! That's not nice."

The mother called the doctor, and the doctor said,

"No more penguins slipping on the ice!"

Four little penguins sliding near a tree.

One fell into the icy sea!

The mother called the doctor, and the doctor said,

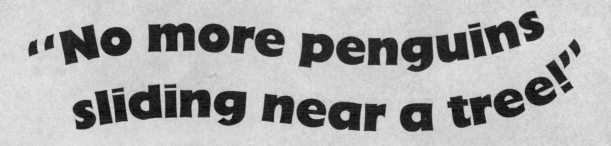

"No more penguins
sliding near a tree!"

Three little penguins skating all around.

One flew up and then fell down!

The mother called the doctor, and the doctor said,

"No more penguins skating all around!"

Two little penguins playing on a hill.

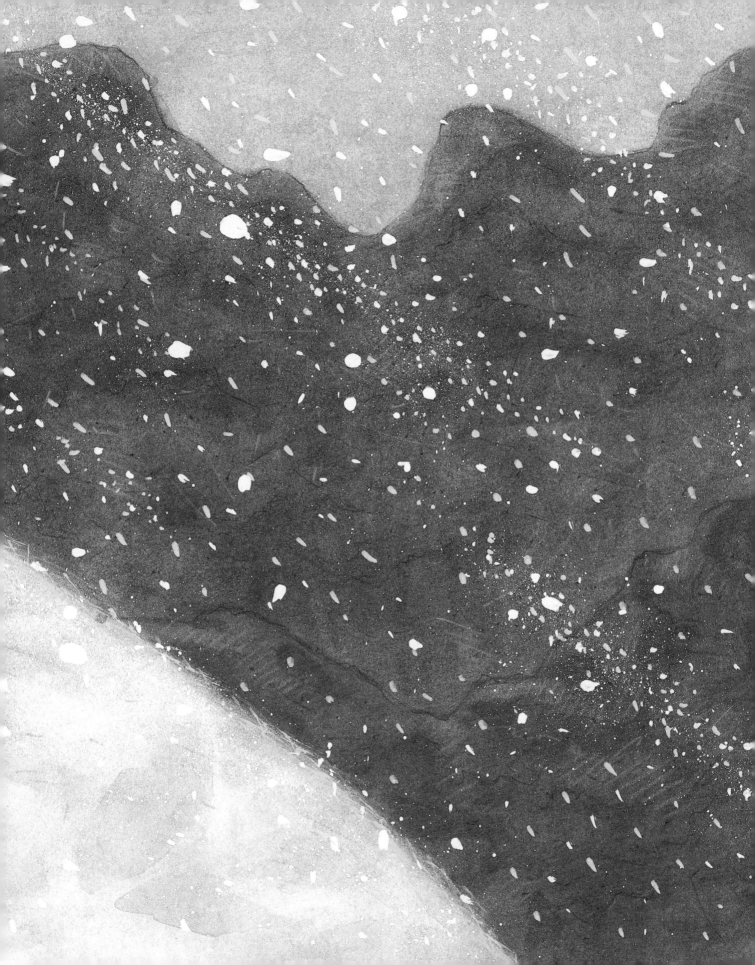

One slipped off and banged her bill.

The mother called the doctor, and the doctor said,

"No more penguins playing on a hill!"

One little penguin jumping very high

Broke the ice and began to cry.

The mother called the doctor, and the doctor said,

"No more penguins jumping very high!"

Now there's…
No little penguins having any fun.
No little penguins, not even one.

The mother called the doctor, and the doctor said,

"Let those penguins have some fun!"